Jimbo, origi... ... stowaway, but Captain Roger allowed him to join the crew as ship's boy

Flashfork, ship's cook. He is no master chef but the crew rarely complain; he's a hot-tempered man, armed with a cutlass and a rolling pin!

Anne, the daughter of Bessie, landlady at the inn on Pirate Island. She is a fearless pirate and loves to take part in Darkshark's adventures whenever she can

Spinoza, the mischievous ship's monkey and **Popsy**, Captain Roger's faithful and very talkative parrot

On the large island of Sabatina, somewhere in the Tropical Sea, lives Governor Broadside with his sister Aunt Prudence and niece Camilla.

Life is never quiet for the Governor and his men as they try to keep law and order in the territory. The seas are full of pirates, pirate ships and pirate adventures, with Captain Roger, Bo'sun Will and the crew of the Darkshark *constantly pitting their wits against their arch enemies, Captain Foul and the crew of the* Barracuda.

British Library Cataloguing in Publication Data

Grant, John, *1930-*
    The royal visit.
    I. Title   II. Davis, Jon   III. Series
    823.914[J]
    ISBN 0-7214-1346-3

First edition

Published by Ladybird Books Ltd Loughborough Leicestershire UK
Ladybird Books Inc Auburn Maine 04210 USA

® LEGO is a registered trademark belonging to the LEGO Group and is used here
    by special permission.
© LEGO GROUP MCMXC
© LADYBIRD BOOKS LTD MCMXC

Printed in England (3)

The Royal Visit

by JOHN GRANT
illustrated by JON DAVIS

Ladybird Books

It was a pleasant afternoon at sea. Aboard *Darkshark* Bo'sun Will lay on his bunk reading a book. In his cabin, Captain Roger was taking afternoon tea. He was pouring himself a second cup when, with a crash, a cannonball hurtled through the cabin window! The tea things flew in all directions as the cannonball crashed out through the window opposite!

At the same time a voice shouted, "*DARKSHARK* AHOY! HEAVE TO! I'M COMING ABOARD!"

Captain Roger rushed on deck. A sinister-looking ship was bearing down on *Darkshark*. It was Governor Broadside's flagship *Ironram*! And the Governor himself stood on the poop deck with a speaking trumpet.

"HEAVE TO! IN THE NAME OF THE KING!" shouted the Governor.

"Not likely!" cried Roger. "All hands! Set every sail we've got! If he wants me, he'll have to catch me first!"

Will ran up. "We can't outrun *Ironram*," he said. "Nobody can. She's the fastest ship in the Islands."

"Not outrun. Outsmart," said Roger. "Look over there." Will looked. The sky was becoming hazy. Thick fog was coming down on the sea. "We'll give them the slip in the fog," said Roger.

There was a bang and another cannonball whizzed over *Darkshark*'s bow. Then they were safely into the fog.

The fog lasted until evening. When it lifted there was no sign of Governor Broadside or his ship. Captain Roger called the crew on deck. "What I should like to know," he shouted, "is how *Ironram* managed to sneak up like that. Who was on look-out?"

"Rummy," said one of the pirates.

"Did someone call my name?" came Rummy's voice. He looked down from the crow's nest, rubbing his eyes.

"Sorry. I must have fallen asleep."

Captain Roger jumped up and down with rage. "And why didn't *you* see them coming?" he shouted at Will.

"I was in my cabin," said Will, "reading."

"That's all I need!" cried the Captain. "A first mate who falls asleep, and a bo'sun who's a bookworm!"

A few days later *Darkshark* dropped anchor off Pirates' Nest.

"It's very quiet," said Will, as they went ashore. "I think there's something wrong. Why does everyone look so miserable?"

The pirates entered the "Keg and Cutlass". But there was no cheery bustle. The customers looked gloomily into their glasses. Even Bessie the landlady looked unhappy.

"The King is coming on a state visit," she said. "The Governor is to receive His Majesty in full dress uniform, which includes his badge of office. But... he's lost it! The badge, that is!"

"And the Governor thinks one of us has taken his badge!" cried Captain Foul.

"That explains a lot," said Roger. "But why all the fuss over a fancy badge on a coloured ribbon? Can't he wear something else?"

"It is a very serious offence for a Governor to lose his badge," said Will. "I read that in a book. A Governor who loses his badge is likely to lose his position... or even his head! So Governor Broadside will be a very worried man. That's why he's making things hard for us all."

"Then we must help him to find it!" cried Captain Roger. "We might lose a bad Governor... and get another who's even worse!"

That very day, Captain Roger called a meeting of all the pirate captains in the "Keg and Cutlass".

"These are troubled times," he said. "We must find Broadside's badge, which means no raiding, looting, plank walking or keel hauling until it's found. All in favour say 'Aye'."

"AYE!" shouted the pirate captains.

Bessie served drinks. "I don't see Captain Jonah here," she said.

"He's probably run aground or been dismasted or something else unlucky," said one of the pirates. "Last week, in the dark, he mistook Port Royal for Pirates' Nest. He just managed to escape... the first piece of luck he's ever had!"

Back on board *Darkshark*, Bessie's daughter Anne was feeding nuts to Popsy.

"Why," she asked Will, "do pirates always have parrots?"

"They don't," said Will. "Captain Jonah of the schooner *Hesperus* is so bad at pirating that he can't afford a parrot. He has a pet jackdaw, but I heard that it flew away when *Hesperus* was fighting her way out of Port Royal last week."

Will thought for a moment. Then he jumped up. "That's given me an idea!" he cried. He dashed down to his cabin and began rummaging among his books.

Minutes later
Will was back
on deck. "I think
I know where the
Governor's badge might be, Captain."

Roger listened as Will explained. Then
he laughed and laughed. "What a crazy
idea!" he exclaimed.

"Has anyone got a better idea… or any idea for that matter?" asked Will. And the Captain had to admit that no one had.

"Right," said Will, "in that case I think the sooner we set off to look for Captain Jonah and the *Hesperus* the better."

Darkshark set sail. Three days later they found *Hesperus* anchored in a sheltered bay.

The crew of the *Hesperus* were making repairs. Captain Jonah had had a collision with a large whale.

Jonah was pleased to have visitors. Most people avoided him in case his bad luck was catching. Will explained about the missing badge of office.

"Serves him right," said Jonah. "Anyone could sail into the wrong harbour. He didn't need to go shooting cannons at us. Diogenes, poor bird, got such a fright. He flew away. He's back now, safely in his barrel."

Captain Roger frowned. Will explained. "Diogenes is a jackdaw. I've done some reading and..." He broke off and turned to Captain Jonah. "Where is Diogenes' barrel? I'd like to examine it."

"Help yourself," said Jonah. "It's up there on the quarterdeck."

The others hung back. But Anne followed Will as he picked his way carefully among worm-eaten timbers, loose planks, and frayed rigging. *Hesperus* was a floating wreck!

Up on the quarterdeck a small barrel was wedged on its side beside the ship's wheel. Tattered wisps of straw and other nesting material hung out of one end.

"Here, Diogenes! Good bird!" said Will, stooping to look inside the barrel. But a loose plank moved under his foot. He stumbled and lost his balance... and fell headlong on top of the barrel! The barrel burst and a screeching Diogenes flew up into the rigging.

Anne burst out laughing. But Will ignored her and searched with his fingers among the broken wood and straw. He found a few brass buttons, some brightly coloured shells, a silver tea spoon... and something else... a length of slightly chewed-looking ribbon. And from the ribbon hung a dirty, but still sparkling, gold badge set with precious stones.

Everyone was speechless.

"It's Governor Broadside's badge of office!" said Captain Jonah at last. "How did you know it was there?"

"I didn't," said Will. "Not for certain. But I knew that Diogenes had flown ashore near Port Royal. And in one of my books there's a poem about a jackdaw who stole a diamond ring. They do that sort of thing, you know!"

Darkshark sailed home in triumph. Captain Roger sent word to all the other captains that the badge of office was found, and they could stop looking.

Will made a plan to make sure that the badge reached the Governor safely. He and Anne joined the crew of a fishing boat bound for Port Royal. And very early on the morning of the royal visit, Anne, disguised as a washerwoman, smuggled the badge into Fort Sabre with the Governor's laundry.

A servant found it... and left it lying mysteriously by the Governor's bed, for the Governor to discover when he awoke.

The royal visit was a great success. The King personally shook Governor Broadside by the hand and gave him a medal. That made the Governor very happy. He became his old greedy, lazy and bad-tempered self again. He went back to governing. The pirates were left more or less in peace to carry on pirating. And they all lived happily (more or less) ever after.